All You Need

Howard Schwartz

Illustrated by Jasu Hu

NEAL PORTER BOOKS

HOLIDAY HOUSE / NEW YORK

For my beautiful granddaughter, Ariah —H.S.

For my parents —J.H.

Neal Porter Books

Text copyright © 2022 by Howard Schwartz

Illustrations copyright © 2022 by Jasu Hu

All Rights Reserved

HOLIDAY HOUSE is registered in the U.S. Patent and Trademark Office.

Printed and bound in December 2021 at C & C Offset, Shenzhen, China.

The artwork for this book was made using watercolor.

Book design by Jennifer Browne

www.holidayhouse.com

First Edition

1 3 5 7 9 10 8 6 4 2

Library of Congress Cataloging-in-Publication Data

Names: Schwartz, Howard, 1945– author. | Hu, Jasu, illustrator.

Title: All you need / written by Howard Schwartz ; illustrated by Jasu Hu.

Description: First edition. | New York : Holiday House, 2022. | "A Neal
Porter Book." | Audience: Ages 4 to 8. | Audience: Grades K–1. |
Summary: "A girl grows up to be an accomplished artist in this book
about the small things that lead to a rich and fulfilling life"—
Provided by publisher.

Identifiers: LCCN 2021005498 | ISBN 9780823443291 (hardcover)

Subjects: LCSH: Life—Juvenile fiction. | Quality of life—Juvenile
fiction. | Picture books for children. | CYAC: Life—Fiction. | Quality
of life—Fiction. | LCGFT: Picture books.

Classification: LCC PZ7.S4078 Al 2022 | DDC 813.54 [E]—dc23

LC record available at https://lccn.loc.gov/2021005498

ISBN: 978-0-8234-4329-1 (hardcover)

All you need

is a planet to live on,

a sun to give you light

and warmth,

clouds to gather rain,

seeds to take root,

and trees to clean the air

for you to breathe.

You also need

good food to grow,

fresh water

to quench your thirst,

and plenty of sleep.

Finally, you need a land

where you are welcome,

someone to watch over you,

words to share your thoughts,

a hand
to write those
words down,

亲爱的
我很开
找到了

and a beating heart.

A Note from the Author

The words of *All You Need* first came to me as a poem. I was thinking about the essentials everyone needs in order to thrive in this world—air, water, food, sleep, and, of course, a planet to live on. I'm grateful to my publisher, Neal Porter, who realized that all children need to recognize these essential things in order to help them understand and appreciate the miracle of being alive. He also knew of a wonderful young Chinese artist, Jasu Hu, whose watercolors are as light as air and seem to come alive on the page. She told the story of the young child from her own perspective—it is, after all, a universal story. I'm stunned by her astonishing illustrations, and very grateful, and I know you will be too.

From my beating heart to yours,
Howard Schwartz

A Note from the Artist

I spent parts of my childhood in the countryside of Hunan, China. I remember it as a wonderful time. When I was little, I would often be alone in a daze, looking at the sky, the sun, and the rain, and thinking about the question, "What are they to me?" This was still the case when I left my home country to explore new environments as an adult. When my editor, Neal Porter, handed the manuscript for Howard's *All You Need* to me, I felt the connection to nature, dreams, and love through this poem. It evoked my childhood memories and also how much I missed my parents. This is why I chose to use my own perspective and experience as inspiration to create the story for this book.

If you look closely, you will find that the little girl is gradually growing, and the scene is gradually changing along with the seasons. But there is a "friend" who is always with her—a swallow. In Chinese culture, the swallow is a messenger that brings happiness and is a symbol of homecoming. My work on this book began in New York in 2019. Due to the travel restrictions caused by COVID-19 in 2020, I found myself stranded in Serbia for three months, where I continued my work. Though I couldn't return to the United States, I was able to return to my parents in Nanjing, and that became a real homecoming, and then back to Hunan, where I finished all of the watercolor paintings for this book, inspired by the area where I grew up. I think that was a blessing in disguise, and I am so grateful for it.

My thanks to Howard and all the beautiful people who made this unique collaboration come together. I hope this book allows you to feel all the forms of love in this world, as well as your own warm beating heart.

Jasu Hu